DAMIAN DROOTH SUPERSLEUTH

THE GRAFFITI MYSTERY

by Barbara Mitchelhill

illustrated by Tony Ross

STONE ARCH BOOKS
www.stonearchbooks.com

J FIC
MIT
Mystery

First published in the United States in 2009
by Stone Arch Books
151 Good Counsel Drive, P.O. Box 669
Mankato, Minnesota 56002
www.stonearchbooks.com

First published in 2007
by Andersen Press Ltd, London

Text copyright © 2007 Barbara Mitchelhill
Illustrations copyright © 2007 Tony Ross

The right of Barbara Mitchelhill to be identified as the author
of this work has been asserted by her in accordance
with the Copyright, Designs and Patent Act 1988.

Library of Congress Cataloging-in-Publication Data
Mitchelhill, Barbara.
    [Serious graffiti]
    The Graffiti Mystery / by Barbara Mitchelhill; illustrated by
Tony Ross.
    p. cm. — (Pathway Books) (Damian Drooth Supersleuth)
    Originally published: Serious graffiti. London: Andersen, 2007.
    ISBN 978-1-4342-1215-3 (library binding)
    [1. Mystery and detective stories. 2. Vandalism—Fiction.
3. Graffiti—Fiction.] I. Ross, Tony, ill. II. Title.
PZ7.M697Gr 2009
[Fic]—dc22   2 4 3 6 0 5 7 3 5   2008031824

Summary: Vandals have struck at Damian's school — someone has been
spray-painting graffiti in the boys' bathroom! To make matters worse, the
vandals can't even spell. If the crooks aren't stopped, the whole school
will be on cleaning duty. Damian knows he's the school's only hope of
solving this bad spell of crime!

Creative Director: Heather Kindseth
Graphic Designer: Emily Harris

For Max and Tom Scott and their mum and dad, with much love, B. M.

1 2 3 4 5 6 14 13 12 11 10 09

Printed in the United States of America

Table of Contents

Chapter 1

You probably know my name. I'm Damian Drooth, Supersleuth and Ace Detective. I've solved lots of crimes, but let me tell you about one that happened at our school.

It was really exciting. The principal couldn't solve it. The police couldn't solve it. But in the end, I solved it.

I first heard about the crime last Thursday during math. The principal, Mr. Spratt, came marching into our classroom. I could tell that he was in a bad mood. When he's in a bad mood, he looks over his glasses, and he was peering over them now.

"I have something serious to tell you all," he said to the class. "Someone has sprayed paint on the walls of the boys' bathroom. This graffiti is disgraceful. We just had that bathroom painted. Now it will have to be painted again."

He stared at everybody with his beady black eyes. Then he went on. "I want the person responsible for the graffiti to come to my office before the end of school tomorrow."

He paused and looked at us angrily. Then he added, "Otherwise, the whole school is going to be punished."

A gasp rippled around the room.

"That's not fair," Winston said. I thought that was very brave of him. "We didn't do it," he added.

Mr. Spratt said, "I don't care if it's fair or not. Somebody must know who did the graffiti. It's up to you to come and tell me who that person was."

Then he left, slamming the door behind him.

We were all stunned. We sat there
feeling really worried, wondering how
he would punish us. Would he stop all
basketball games for the next year?
Would he make us come to school on
Saturdays? Would he make us write a
million essays?

Our teacher, Mr. Grimethorpe, looked very worried. He always looked worried, but today he looked even worse. "This is terrible news. Terrible news," he said, shaking his head.

That's when Todd stood up and said, "Don't worry, Mr. Grimethorpe. We'll find out who did it."

Mr. Grimethorpe sighed. "And how will you do that, Todd?" he asked.

"We have Damian," Todd said. "It won't take him long to track down this criminal."

The eyes of the whole class were on me.

"Maybe," I said mysteriously. "I'll have to check out the crime scene and look for clues. It could take a while."

The kids started to ask all kinds of questions. "Where will you look first?" "How do you know a clue when you see it?" "What if the criminal's dangerous?"

They went on and on until Mr. Grimethorpe clapped his hands for quiet.

After that, our class discussed graffiti. That was fine with me, because it meant we weren't doing math. Just as it was getting interesting, Mr. Grimethorpe decided we had to get back to work.

I really didn't feel like doing math. "If you want, I can go take a look at the crime scene now," I said. "I need to look for clues as soon as possible."

Mr. Grimethorpe gave me a funny look. "It can wait, Damian," he said. "Get on with your work."

I didn't think this was a good idea. All this time, kids could be messing with the crime scene. I needed to examine it soon.

I put my head down on the desk, pretending to write. Two minutes later, I stood up. I hopped from one foot to the other and waved my hand in the air until Mr. Grimethorpe saw me.

"What is it, Damian?" he asked.

"I need to go to the bathroom," I said.

Mr. Grimethorpe frowned. "You're making it up," he said.

I was shocked. "No!" I said. "I can't wait. I really have to go!"

He didn't look pleased. "Oh, fine," he said. "But hurry up."

I headed for the door. Before I opened it, I turned around.

"Can Winston come with me?" I asked. "I'm not feeling very well."

"No," said Mr. Grimethorpe. "Winston has work to do."

"What about Harry?" I asked.

"Harry has work to do too!" Mr. Grimethorpe said.

"Todd?" I asked.

"NO! NO! NO!" my teacher shouted, slamming his hand on the desk. "Go now, Damian. Be back in five minutes or you're in trouble."

Five minutes? That was not much time for one person to check out the graffiti and look for clues. I raced down the hall, hoping that the crime scene had not been ruined.

Chapter 2

At recess, my trainee detectives, Harry, Todd, and Winston, were waiting for me.

"What was it like, Damian?" Todd asked.

"Terrible," I said. "You've never seen anything like it."

"Tell us," Harry said. "What did the graffiti say?"

"It said GET LOST SPRAT!" I whispered.

My friends looked shocked.

"They spelled "Spratt" with one T instead of two," I said. "And they wrote the S's backward."

I had found other clues, too. I pulled a piece of toilet paper out of my pocket, opened it up, and showed them some red flakes.

"What's that?" Winston asked.

"Paint," I said. "I scraped it off the graffiti. Detectives always do that kind of stuff."

"How does that help?" Winston asked.

"Now I can tell what kind of paint the criminal used," I explained.

"So what?" Harry asked.

"So now I can go to the paint store and match it," I said.

I pulled another piece of paper out of my pocket. This one contained a scraping of green paint. "See? He used two colors," I said. "Now I'll buy two cans of spray paint, the same ones the criminal used."

"Why?" Winston asked.

"I have a plan," I said.

I explained it as carefully as I could. "I will take the cans of spray paint to the boys' bathroom and leave them on the floor," I said.

They were all standing with their mouths wide open. I could tell that they didn't understand how I was going to solve the crime. That's because they weren't fully trained yet.

"You see," I said, "when the criminal goes into the bathroom, he'll spot the cans. He'll think he left them there when he did the graffiti. So he'll pick them up and run for it."

"But how will we know?" Todd asked.

"We will keep watch in the bathroom," I said. "There are four of us. We'll take turns, so that Mr. Grimethorpe doesn't get suspicious while we work on the case."

Harry frowned at me. "You have to be joking, Damian," he said. "That won't work. It's the stupidest idea I've ever heard."

"Yeah," said Winston. "Anybody could walk in and pick up the cans. It doesn't make them a criminal."

I tried to explain it, but it was no use. They wouldn't go along with my plan.

So I came up with another one. This one was even better. It was definitely going to work.

"Okay, then we'll hold a competition," I said. "All the kids will have to write something. We'll look for the person who writes their S's backward and spells Spratt with one T. Find the writer and you'll find the kid who did the graffiti."

I had to quickly make them see that this was our only chance of solving the crime. Recess was over in twenty minutes.

We carried a table from the art room around to the back of the bike shed. I wrote a poster and stuck it on the wall.

"I still don't see how this will work, Damian," said Harry. "We don't even have a prize."

"We'll worry about that later," I said. I was busy writing the questions on a large piece of paper.

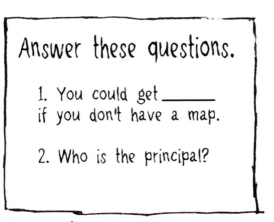

Answer these questions.

1. You could get _____
if you don't have a map.

2. Who is the principal?

Notice how I tricked them into writing the words that had been written on the bathroom walls? That was a stroke of genius.

The news about the competition went around the playground like wildfire. Soon we were surrounded by kids dying to enter the contest.

We tore pages from our notebooks and gave each person a piece. When we ran out of paper, I used my homework book. I could always tell Mr. Grimethorpe that I'd lost it.

When everyone was done writing, we collected the papers. Then some kid asked, "What's the prize, Damian?"

I winked. "You'll just have to wait and see," I said.

"You're a liar," somebody shouted. "I bet there isn't a prize."

After that, it got a little out of hand. Some of the boys started a fight. Then some of the girls joined in. Luckily, the bell rang then and we had to go inside.

All that mattered was that we had the pieces of paper. The evidence was in the writing. Every detective knows that the evidence is the most important thing.

After school, we would check the papers. Then we would find out who had sprayed graffiti on the bathroom wall.

Chapter 3

We went to the park after school. Lavender, who is Todd's sister, came along to help. We looked at all of the contest entries, checking the writing.

Before long, Winston jumped up, waving a paper in the air. "I've got it!" he yelled. "This one spelled Spratt with one T."

"Who did it?" Todd asked.

"George Johnson!" Winston said.

"Whoa!" said Harry. "I always thought he was shy."

"Just a good cover-up," I explained. "Criminals are like that."

Winston passed the paper to me and I examined it. But I could tell right away that George Johnson was not guilty.

"How do you know?" Winston asked.

"Because the S isn't backward. The graffiti writer wrote his S's backward, remember?" I said.

Winston looked disappointed. I had to make him feel better. "Good try, Winston," I said.

We kept looking at the pieces of paper. Todd found another one with the wrong spelling of Spratt. Then Harry found one. Then Lavender found two more.

I was disgusted. "Doesn't anybody know how to spell it?" I asked.

Finally, we made a pile of all the people who couldn't spell the principal's name but who knew how to write an S. That left fifteen papers to look at. We were exhausted.

Luckily, Todd had some chips in his backpack. We took a break.

When we were ready to begin again, I reminded them of the clues they were looking for. You have to make things really clear when you're dealing with trainee detectives.

We had been searching for only a few minutes when Lavender said, "I got it, Damian. I got the criminal!" She went crazy. She was leaping up and down as if she was on a trampoline.

I went to look at the paper she was waving. She was right. The person had spelled Spratt wrong and the S's were backward.

"Good job, Lavender!" I said. I looked at the name on the paper. "Daisy Parker. She's in your class, isn't she, Lavender?" I asked.

"Yes, she is," Lavender said.

"I bet you are surprised that Daisy is a criminal," I said. "I'm surprised she even went into the boys' bathroom. I'm also surprised that she could spray those great big letters across the bathroom wall. She's only six."

"Yes," said Lavender. "And she's my best friend." Then she stuck out her bottom lip and burst into tears.

Besides Lavender crying, my brilliant plan had worked just as I expected. I had tracked down the girl who had ruined the newly painted walls. I was a great detective!

"I'll have to report her to the principal," I said. "He'll probably have to call the police."

Lavender's wails grew louder and louder. Even if Daisy was her best friend, I would have to tell the principal what I had found.

"No, you won't have to report Daisy to the principal," said Harry.

I was shocked when he said that. "What do you mean?" I asked. "We have evidence. Daisy Parker is the criminal, and that's that."

"Daisy Parker isn't the only one who can't spell and can't write her S's," Harry said. He held a paper in his hand. "Here's James O'Boyle's. It's the same."

This made things difficult. Now there were two suspects. When we were done looking at all the papers, we had found another four suspects.

Lavender stopped crying as soon as she realized that Daisy Parker was no longer the main suspect. That was a good thing, because her crying was giving me a headache.

"So what now?" asked Todd.

"Well," said Harry, "we can't prove any of these six did it. It's hopeless. I'm going home."

So that was it. They all went home.

I stayed at the park, trying to think of another plan. But it was no good. I was too exhausted to come up with any new ideas.

So I decided to go back to my first one. My friends thought it was a terrible idea, but I didn't. I would go to the store and find paint that matched the paint I had scraped from the walls. It was my only hope.

Chapter 4

As soon as I had seen the graffiti that morning, I knew it had not been done with ordinary paint. (I have a trained eye for that kind of thing.)

So when I went into the paint store, there was only one kind of paint that I was looking for — spray paint.

Of course, there was every type of paint you can imagine. It was stacked high. There were rows and rows of it. The spray cans were in Aisle 3.

Unfortunately, there was a woman in that aisle stacking shelves. She was wearing a bright yellow sweatshirt with the store's name printed on the front. She had her eye on me as soon as I got near the spray paint.

"Can I help you?" she asked.

I was busy studying the colors. I was trying to match them up to the flakes of paint I'd taken from the bathroom.

I shook my head. "No thanks," I said. "I'm fine."

She pretended she had finished her work and walked down the aisle to stand next to me.

"So, you're buying cans of spray paint, are you?" she asked.

I looked at her but said nothing.

The saleswoman stood next to me with her hands on her hips. "You wouldn't be thinking of doing graffiti, would you?" she asked.

Now I was really mad. "No, I wouldn't," I said. "I'm buying some paint for my mom, if you must know. She wants to paint our kitchen cabinets."

"Red and green? That's a little bright," the woman said.

"It's the new trend," I said.

She didn't believe me. "You're a little young to be here all alone, aren't you?" she asked.

I had had enough! I was about to grab the paint and make a run for it when my neighbor Mrs. Robertson came around the corner, pushing a cart.

"Hello, Damian," she said. "What are you doing here?"

"Do you know this boy?" the woman asked angrily.

Mrs. Robertson is a great lady. She just smiled and said, "Yes, I know Damian. He lives next door to me."

"Does he?" the lady said. "Well, I think he was trying to steal some cans of paint." She leaned forward in a sneaky kind of way and said, "I suspect that he's one of those children who goes around spray-painting graffiti on walls."

You should have seen Mrs. Robertson's face. She was really mad.

"Damian? Graffiti?" she said. "No way. I'm sure he has a very good reason for wanting to buy the paint."

Mrs. Robertson turned away from the woman and said, "Pick up the cans you need, Damian, and we'll go to the checkout. We're not going to stand here to be insulted."

"Okay," I said as I reached for the paint. "Mom's at home waiting for this," I added. That wasn't actually true, but the saleswoman didn't know that.

She shouldn't have accused me of stealing, that's what I say.

Anyway, I gave her one of my special innocent smiles and walked away, following Mrs. Robertson and her cart.

It wasn't until we were standing in the line at the checkout that I realized that I didn't have any money. What could I do? I couldn't let my plan fail at this stage.

My brain started working right away. It didn't take long for it to come up with a great idea.

"Oh no!" I said really loudly. Then I said, "OH NO!" even louder.

Mrs. Robertson, who was taking some wallpaper out of her cart, turned around to see what was the matter. "Is something wrong, Damian?" she asked.

I stood there feeling around in my pockets. "There's a hole in my pocket and my money fell out," I said. I shook my head and frowned. "It's all my fault. I should have noticed," I added sadly. "Now I can't pay for the paint."

Mrs. Robertson smiled. "No problem, Damian," she said. "I'll pay. You can pay me back when you get home."

My plan had worked. I smiled and said, "That's great! Thanks, Mrs. Robertson." Then I said, "But you won't mention it to Mom, will you? She'll get upset if she knows I lost the money she gave me."

"Trust me," said Mrs. Robertson. She winked at me. "I promise I won't say a word."

When I got home, Mom was in one of her bad moods — just because I was a few minutes later than usual. She asked, "Where have you been, Damian? Why are you late? What have you been up to?"

I had to keep my mouth zipped. I didn't want to ruin the case. I just ran to my room, got the money I owed Mrs. Robertson, and ran back out.

Besides the Mom problem, things were going well. Now that I had the paint, everything was on track to solve the graffiti crime. I only had to wait until the next morning to put the plan into action.

Chapter 5

Things happened faster than I
expected the next day. I got to school
early (with the cans of paint in my
pockets, of course).

But the police were there before me.
There was a police car parked in front of
the school. A policewoman was standing
in front of the teachers' parking lot,
trying to block it off with some yellow
tape.

I thought I'd better check out what was going on, so I walked in through the main gate.

"I'm Damian Drooth, Ace Detective," I said. I pulled my detective's badge out of my pocket and waved it at her. "Is this a crime scene?" I asked.

The police officer hardly looked at my badge. She wasn't interested.

Maybe I needed to make a new badge. The cardboard on my old one was starting to curl up at the edges.

"I'm very experienced in solving crimes," I added. "Just ask your boss, Inspector Crockitt. I might be able to help."

The police officer raised one eyebrow and smirked. "I don't think so," she said. "Now please go and play your detective games in the playground. I'm doing serious work here."

I get really mad when people treat me like a kid. I can't stand it.

The police officer was probably new to the area. She didn't know I was a local hero. Inspector Crockitt should really tell new officers about me, if you ask me.

I could see that there was no point in talking to the police officer, so I pretended to walk away. But really, I slipped around the back and walked up to the parking lot from the other side. The policewoman was too busy, so she didn't see me.

What I saw shocked me!

There was the principal's car. It was silver and shiny and brand new. SPRAT GO HOME had been sprayed in red paint along the side.

This was disgusting! Not only had someone messed up the principal's car, but they couldn't even spell his name right.

My detective skills told me that it had probably been the same person who spray-painted the bathroom wall. I was almost sure of it.

I looked closer at the car. The hood had more paint on it. It was even worse. There was a drawing of Spratt's face. The person had made him look bug-eyed, and added some Dracula fangs painted in green.

This was serious graffiti. The principal must be really mad. No wonder he had called the police.

I sneaked up to the car. First, I touched the hood of the car. The green paint was still wet. Bingo! The criminal couldn't be far away. Next, I hurried along to look at the red writing. It was wet too.

Then I found the most important clue of all! A footprint, in red paint. I couldn't believe my luck! I knew I had to make a sketch of it right away.

I had used all the pages in my notebook for the competition the day before, so I had to think of something else to use. Luckily, I was wearing a white shirt. I pulled the front of my shirt out, spread it on the car, and quickly sketched the footprint on it.

I finished up my drawing and started to put my pen back in my pocket. Just then, I felt a big hand grab onto my shoulder.

"What exactly do you think you are doing?" a man's voice asked. "Are you hoping to do some more graffiti? Well, too bad, kid."

I spun around and saw a large policeman with mean eyes. He was glaring at me angrily.

"I'm Damian Drooth, Ace Detective," I explained. "And I'm here to help you solve the graffiti crime."

He gave a loud laugh that sounded like he didn't believe me. "You'd better come with me," he said. "We'll see what the principal says about you."

He practically dragged me into school and down the hall to Mr. Spratt's office.

"Here's the criminal," the policeman said as he shoved me through the door.

When Mr. Spratt saw me, his jaw dropped. I guessed he was shocked to see that the school's most famous student had been arrested.

I waited for him to shout something like, "You've made a terrible mistake, officer!" But he didn't.

Instead, Mr. Spratt said, "Damian Drooth! So it was you who spray-painted my car!"

I couldn't believe it. How could he think that I would do such a thing?

"No!" I said. "I didn't!"

The policeman grabbed my hands. He held them out for Mr. Spratt to see.

"Just look," the police officer said. "There's paint all over him. Isn't that the same as the paint that's been sprayed on your car?"

Mr. Spratt nodded. "I'm afraid it is," he said.

It was true that I had gotten a small amount of red and green paint on my fingers, and some on the front of my shirt. I couldn't deny that.

But I had gotten it on me while searching for clues! Why didn't they understand that?

I turned around to explain this to the policeman. As I turned, one of the cans of paint fell out of my pocket.

"Aha!" the officer said. He picked up the can and put it in a plastic bag. "More evidence."

Mr. Spratt stood up. "We'll have to call his mother before you can arrest him," he told the police officer. "We'll find a room where he can wait until she arrives."

He looked at me, his mouth drooping at the corners. "This is a sad, sad day for the school, Damian," he said.

So that was how I got locked in the nurse's office, wondering how I could escape and find the real criminal.

Chapter 6

The security in our school was less than perfect. It was easy to unlock the window and open it.

It was really high up, though, and I didn't like the idea of dropping onto concrete and breaking both legs and possibly an arm. No way.

Luckily, while I was planning what to do, Harry and Winston came running through the school gates.

I made the sound of an owl to attract their attention. Spies do this when they don't want anybody to notice them. But Harry and Winston weren't listening for owls, so they didn't even look my way.

I had to yell, "Harry! Winston! Over here!" They came running to the window.

"What are you doing, Damian?" Harry asked.

"They think I did the graffiti," I said. "They'll probably put me in prison."

"Whoa!" Winston said.

"Help me down!" I told them.

I got them to stand under the window with their arms spread against the wall. Then I slid out and put my feet on their shoulders.

It worked until Winston's knees collapsed and we landed in a heap.

"Now I'll sneak into the school," I said. "Then I'll tell the name of the real crook to the whole school."

"Do you know who did it?" Winston asked.

"No, but I will soon," I told them.

I had been smart enough to borrow a white outfit from the nurse's office. Once I put on my sunglasses and hat, no one would know who I was.

It was bad luck that the policeman and Mom walked up right then.

"Damian!" Mom screeched. "What do you think you're doing?"

"Run for it!" I yelled.

I raced across the playground and
burst into the school, followed by Harry,
Winston, Mom, and the policeman.

Mr. Spratt was giving one of his boring
speeches. Inspector Crockitt was next to
him. I guessed he was there to talk to the
kids about the terrible crime of spraying
paint.

"Damian Drooth!" shouted Mr. Spratt. "How did you get out? Mr. Grimethorpe, take him back to the nurse's office."

Inspector Crockitt said, "Let him stay and tell us why he's here, Mr. Spratt. I have learned that Damian has a unique way of looking at crime."

It was good to hear that. I stepped forward to the front of the room. "I know who has been doing all this graffiti," I announced. "I have the evidence here."

I pulled out the front of my shirt so they could see the drawing of the footprint. There were gasps around the hall. Even Inspector Crockitt looked amazed.

I turned to Mr. Spratt. "I would like to see the bottoms of everybody's shoes," I said.

Mr. Spratt started to shake his head. Inspector Crockitt looked at him and nodded.

"Oh, fine," said Mr. Spratt. "Children, please stretch your legs out so that we can see the bottom of your shoes."

It didn't take long. I spotted it right away. "Barney Scott," I shouted. "You are the criminal." The soles of his shoes matched my sketch. Plus, one of them was covered in red paint.

Barney tried to escape. He jumped up and ran for the door, but Todd, Harry, and Winston were too fast for him. They tackled him.

The graffiti mystery had been solved.

Chapter 7

Back in the principal's office, I talked to Inspector Crockitt. Of course, he would need more proof than some red paint on Barney's shoe and a sketch on my shirt.

"I've got something else," I said. I pulled the six competition entries out of my pocket.

"What's this, Damian?" the inspector asked.

I explained, "We did a writing test yesterday. Here are the ones that matched the graffiti. This is all the evidence you'll need."

He was shocked when I handed him the papers. He paged through them, looking at the names on each one.

"Here's Barney Scott's!" Inspector Crockitt said. "You're right! He can't spell Spratt and he doesn't know how to write an S. Good work, Damian."

Sometimes the police need help in solving crimes. I do my best.

The police weren't the only ones who were grateful. "You're a credit to the school," Mr. Spratt said.

Or he said something like that, anyway. He gave me a box of candy as a thank you.

I was looking forward to eating the candy when I got home. I planned to save the caramel ones for the others. After all, they did help.

The kids who had entered the competition were in a bad mood.

"What about the prize?" they asked
me. "You promised there'd be a prize."

I tried to get away from them, but
it didn't work. They kept shouting and
poking me and bugging me. So finally, I
said, "Daisy Parker is the winner, and the
prize is a box of candy."

That shut them up.

Daisy was Lavender's best friend.
I had no choice but to hand her the
chocolates.

"Oh, thank you, Damian!" she said. "I've never won a prize before."

She was a nice kid. I wondered if she would like to train with the rest of the trainee detectives.

"You can come to the detective school if you want, Daisy," I said.

"Can I really, Damian?" she said. "Can I be a detective like Lavender?"

"We'll see," I said. "We're all meeting after school to discuss the graffiti case. Bring your chocolates. New members of the Detective Club always bring something to eat. It's a tradition."

That day after school, we all met in the shed in my back yard. Daisy remembered to bring her chocolates. That was good.

Daisy was happy to be invited.

Lavender was happy to have her best friend there.

Harry, Todd, and Winston were happy that the crime was solved.

The only person who wasn't happy was my mom. She was mad.

"How do you do it, Damian?" she moaned. "Just look at your pants. They're ripped right down the leg. And your new shirt is covered in paint. It's ruined! Ruined! Why can't you stay out of trouble?"

I often wonder if Mom will ever see that her son is a true genius. Maybe one day. Maybe.

About the Author

Barbara Mitchelhill started writing when she was seven years old. She says, "When I was eight or nine, I used to pretend I was a detective, just like Damian. My friend Liz and I used to watch people walking down our street and we would write clues in our notebooks. I don't remember catching any criminals!" She has written many books for children. She lives in Staffordshire, England, and writes her books in her wonderful study overlooking fields of sheep. She has a dog named Ella.

About the Illustrator

Tony Ross was born in London in 1938. He has illustrated lots of books, including some by Paula Danziger, Michael Palin, and Roald Dahl. He also writes and illustrates his own books. He has worked as a cartoonist, graphic designer, and art director of an advertising agency. When he was a kid, he wanted to grow up to be a cowboy.

Glossary

crime scene (KRIME SEEN)—the place where a crime took place

criminal (KRIM-uh-nuhl)—someone who commits a crime

evidence (EV-uh-duhnss)—information and facts that help prove something

examine (eg-ZAM-uhn)—look carefully at something

genius (JEEN-yuss)—if you are a genius, you are very smart

graffiti (gruh-FEE-tee)—pictures drawn or words written on walls, cars, or other surfaces. Graffiti is illegal.

responsible (ri-SPON-suh-buhl)—if you are responsible for something, you caused it to happen

suspect (SUH-spekt)—someone thought to be responsible for a crime

suspicious (suh-SPISH-uhss)—if you feel suspicious, you think something is wrong

trainee (tray-NEE)—someone who is learning something

unique (yoo-NEEK)—the only one of its kind

Discussion Questions

1. Graffiti is illegal, but some people consider it an art form. What do you think about graffiti? Do you think it should be legal? Talk about graffiti.

2. Would you want to be one of Damian's trainee detectives? What would be good about it? What would be bad about it? Talk about your reasons.

3. What rules does Damian break in this book? What other ways could he have solved the case?

Writing Prompts

1. Has a crime ever happened at your school? Write about what happened.

2. Damian and his friends solve mysteries together. Write about something that you and your friends like to do together.

3. This book is a mystery story. Write your own mystery story!

Internet Sites

Do you want to know more about subjects related to this book? Or are you interested in learning about other topics? Then check out FactHound, a fun, easy way to find Internet sites.

Our investigative staff has already sniffed out great sites for you!

Here's how to use FactHound:

1. Visit *www.facthound.com*

2. Select your grade level.

3. To learn more about subjects related to this book, type in the book's ISBN number: **9781434212153**.

4. Click the **Fetch It** button.

FactHound will fetch the best Internet sites for you!